PROVOCATION

THE INSECURITY TRIPTYCH
THREE NOVELLAS. THREE SECURITY GUARDS.
THREE NIGHTMARES.

Provocation

Anorexia nervosa survivor Madeleine Kyle embodies twenty-one years of medical intervention; a complex system of internal rules to navigate the dark tides of her fate. When she is stalked by a State Library security guard, Madeleine is pushed to the depths of her unique psyche. In a violent endgame, meaning and motive are as murky as the depths of a river in flood.

The Centre

Zilla Bannich is a dark haired, thick-thighed Polish-Australian misfit on the Gold Coast. As a shopping centre security guard, Zilla is first-on-scene to an incident—a child abandoned, a mother abducted—but falls under suspicion as she clumsily taints the evidence and appears to know the child. *The Centre* explores unspoken truths of girlhood and the erotic passion of belonging, leading us to consider the freedom of love in liminal spaces.

Crawlspace

In 1987, baby Marlene witnesses her father mutilated in a Port Moresby compound invasion, giving rise to a deep psychological scar and a powerful family secret. Twenty-five years later, Marlene finds her perfect match in depressed outer-suburban Brisbane. Andy is a Visa-dependent teenage American escaping his past, and a cyber-security guard who can lay his hands on your money anytime he chooses. An unplanned pregnancy gives urgency to Marlene and Andy's next scam. But who is it that watches from the crawlspace under their humble house of dreams?

PROVOCATION

INSECURITY TRIPTYCH #1

MEG VANN

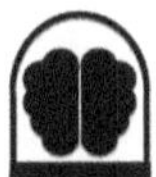

Brain Jar Press
PO Box 6687
Upper Mt Gravatt, QLD, 4122
Australia
www.BrainJarPress.com

Cover design by Peter Ball
Cover Images: Ianxztan/Shutterstock; Bogdan Ionescu/Shutterstock

ISBN: 978-1-922479-03-7

For Helen, in memoriam.

PROVOCATION

Madeleine grips the industrial stapler in her cold palm.

Deep underground, the docks of the gallery and the library are connected. One giant concrete whirlpool of industrial bins, demountable walls, and fallow pallets of props. It was her job to supervise the incoming and outgoing pieces for the children's exhibits in the State Library.

Her dream job.

She stalks around ten foot high dinosaurs and puppet-sized proscenium arches. Pauses, hunkering down behind a towering cage full of flattened boxes. Mould spore catches at the top of her throat, tasting of mangrove funk. She forces a dry, silent swallow. Rests her eyes shut a moment, delicate lids flickering back and forth in a waking REM state, processing her options. Blinks as the oversized double doors swung open. Hydraulic hiss close.

Granger leaned back to adjust the mattress-sized air con unit tucked into a recess at the base of the wide formal stairway. Every morning Madeleine walked up those stairs, and every morning Granger leaned back, fiddling around with knobs that were set right the first time when the building was finished five years ago.

Good morning, he says. Anonymous cadavers, the general public, walk past his long reception counter. Overseas students and family historians check their bags and tag their laptops before being allowed entry into the library proper.

Good morning, they respond.

Madeleine used to say good morning. She used to greet him with the same warm optimism he'd seen her greet everyone, everything.

Not anymore.

He leaned, and fiddled, and checked her out as she tapped a hasty drumroll up the stairs.

A high school girl, warm zebra-stripe skin, venetian blinds in spring sunshine.

Waiting.

Maddi sat up, nudged past her full leather duffel, and headed outside. Maybe if she moved faster, time would get the hint, follow. She paced the small brick-tile courtyard of Moray Clinic, anxiety thickening in her lungs, shoulder blades contracting towards her ears. Paused. Took three long breaths, just like she'd been taught. Perched on the park bench by her door. She gently stroked the cartilage between her nostrils, where once the tube had rubbed her raw. Six weeks as a permanent resident. Then six months as an outpatient, with overnight stays once a week to learn, then demonstrate, her ability to eat, wash, move in a healthy rhythm. That's what they called it. Not a routine, not a regime—a rhythm. Maddi hated it. It was gross, the way the clinic staff talked about her body's every function, every unpredictable need. For years, she had lived by her own simple set of rules.

But still, the gentle pulse of life got into her bones as rhythms do. They drummed wellness into her. She learned to like her wrists and ankles, even to admire the muscular twist of her half-turned waist, instead of always and only seeing fold upon fold of fat. She was a success. A poster girl for the program, although she knew they'd used models for all the posters in the reception.

Her hands rested on the slatted window blinds beside her. She rotated her wrists slowly, watching the sunlight move across her subtle pelt of fine hairs. Her veins still stood out, great vines clinging to her thin bones. Even so, she knew she was well. The sick part of her had been relieved, reduced, reconciled. The compulsion that had become lodged like a touchstone in her belly—making her always full, always empty—had shrunk and all but dissolved.

And this newly brokered peace between her body and her mind gave rise to the sweetest dreams, budding upon the most delicate tendrils of new hope.

A clipboard, swipecard, and the visual equivalent of perfect pitch—they were the tools of her trade. Every day, sometimes for hours, she was down in the dock, taking stock: of books, of inventory, of life. It was no good for her down here, Madeleine knew. No good for her asthma. The place looked clean; cement floors bleached to chalk and leaf-blower bare. But the flood smell lingered, lodged deep in the damp core of the thick concrete walls.

Three stories high, room for ten fully loaded semi-trailers parked two deep and five wide, the transit amphitheatre formed the throbbing heart of the gallery's subterranean network. From there, the rabbit maze led off through a dozen different doors to a hundred different places.

Maddi ticked the last items off her list—five pristine skyblue wheelie bins overflowing with plush Australian animals—and checked her watch. Peered around the dock. Listened carefully. Silence, except for the utility thrum of vent units housed next door. Lance was in the Dock Control office, headphones on, eyes locked on screen. Probably watching a movie. She knew that's how he stayed sane, shut down here all day.

No one else around. She patted a fuzzy Tassie Devil, smiled.

A thick whiff of faecal mould stink and her lungs locked up. Her yoga breathing kicked in automatically, belly-billows slowly pumping long, constricted in- and out- breaths through the wheezing passages in her chest. She glanced at her fingernails, gnawn raw but still pink. Okay for now. When she was little, the heavy courses of steroids that saved her life also left her stunted and plump with bile. From an everyday laughing treasure of a girl, within a few short months she became a dwarven Hitchcock silhouette of misery. As she grew older—never taller, always rounder—she grew accustomed to the daily regime of tests and treatments. She learned her body was a faulty machine. She learned to ignore the beat of her heart, the breath in her lungs, and to simply follow the medical guidelines. Breathe now, medicate now, rest now. No strenuous sport today: here's a note from my doctor.

Oh dear, another one?

Banished to pace around the oval each sweltering day, alone.

As the days and years passed, that level of control had stiffened the flow of her thoughts, made her mind rigid somehow. Dependent on the routine. So when her teenage years hit and the panic attacks started, she'd used the only power she had at hand—her singular focus, her capacity for the steadfast application of a unique set of rules—to find a way out of the wilds of her misery. She shed her Hitchcock silhouette. She stopped her period, cold. Yet so gradual was her transformation, so subtle and cunning were her middle-child ways, that it was nearly three years before anyone noticed. Noticed that the dark receding tide of her fate was killing her.

That was then. Now she lived a normal life, a happy life. She was a miracle.

But.

When she felt stressed, when she got frightened, she could feel the deep water lap at the edges of her mind.

Three slow breaths, stay in the moment, no need to control it. She fingered the smooth plastic button nestled under her shirt, the medical alert button her mother made her wear. The price she paid for her freedom to live away from home. It was already hard to feel grown up when, at twenty-one, she was slight enough to shop in the girls' section.

She just needed a safe place to sit, and be away from the world for a little while. So she picked up a discarded, flattened cardboard box and quietly stepped behind the wheelie bins, hugging the wall. She slunk into the bay, big enough to park six cars, a tiny cove compared to the cavernous dock. A few more steps and she was out of Lance's view. Ten silent steps, then ten more, and she was in the corner of the chamber, and not even security cameras could see her there.

Bit by bit, visit by visit, with innocent questions and shrewd eyes, Maddi had pieced together a complete mental map of the security coverage for the entire dock. There were half a dozen blind spots. She liked this one the best, not for where it was—a bare corner in an often-busy bay—but for where it led.

She ducked through the gap at the bottom of the roller door forming the rear wall of the bay. Probably the maintenance staff were meant to close this tight, after they hauled the storage pallets from the gallery dock to this darkened chamber, but the rightside runner was claggy with putrid rust at about knee height. They usually gave up wrestling the door closed at that point.

She gently frisbeed the cardboard onto the floor beneath the door then lay on it, sliding under and up, fluid as a charmed snake. Rubbed her palms against her clothes, from clavicles down to knees. Her shoulder blades slid down her back, just a fraction. She loved this dual-access space, a shared storage chamber where the gallery and the library tucked away their secrets: failed or outdated displays, awaiting redeployment in regional centres.

Her secret hideaway.

She closed her eyes and ran her hand along the smooth concrete wall, walking forward slowly until her fingertips met modular steel. Opened her eyes to peruse the floor-to-ceiling shelving unit. Her fingers explored the notched silver struts that held heavy bracketed shelves, packed today with large brown boxes. She trailed her fingertips along the shelves that ran along the full length of the side wall, stopping just short of the short climb of stairs up and out into the adjacent gallery dock.

Paused. Her niche. She turned and crouched, tucking herself into the narrow corner formed by the shelves and the gallery landing. Her long backstrap muscles, sinewy from nearly two years of hyper-readiness, unclenched.

Another minute of yoga breathing, and her mind cut adrift, floating free above her. Her hands wandered; caressed the soft hem of her cardigan, smoothed her sandal straps into their buckles. She leaned to one side, pressing her cheek against the cool steel strut of the shelves. It was like sleeping with her eyes open, this delicious sense of privacy, invulnerability, after a life of weakness scrutinised. Her hands kept wandering, seeking out familiar touchstones. The rough edge of that fault in the concrete wall near her right hip, which ran all the way behind the shelves, as far as her arm could comfortably reach. And there, the shadowblack bolt that fastened the whole unit to the wall. It comforted her that one small component could play such a vital role.

As usual, her curious fingers fiddled and turned the bolt, like a child playing with the corner of a beloved blanky. The surface of her mind became smooth and glossy as honey; underneath, shapeless thoughts buzzed a low comforting drone.

A rough rumble broke her out of this delicious meditation. A delivery truck backed up to the chamber, parked, engine running. Tuneless commercial radio bled out from the cab, then blared as the driver opened his door. She peeked through the shelves as a pair of dusty brown boots approached. Her heart pattered quickly in her chest, though she knew she was near invisible in her hiding spot. The owner of the boots tugged at the roller door, budged it open a little, swore. Maddi watched his rumpled dark blue rear mope over to Dock Control.

She pressed back against the wall, tucking her arms around her knees until she was a tiny ball in the corner. The truck chugged blue smoke that stank up the air in her sanctum—she pulled out a tissue, folded it carefully over her mouth and nose, and stayed hidden, waiting impatiently for the driver to return. To climb back into the cab, and send the motorised bin claw into a full fit of hydraulic angst. She was curious to see it happen, the emptying of her private sanctum.

But in a few short minutes her nails were tinged with blue, her lips buzzing with lack of oxygen. Time to go. She peered out, then jumped to her feet, moving silently up the stairs and out to the gallery dock.

Break over, back to work. She'd have to use the gallery dock exit and go right around the river boardwalk, then back through the front door—her back clenched rigid again —past *him*.

The Chubb guys had no time for the inhouse security guards. You could spot the difference straight away: the Chubbies on their feet, stalking the grounds, holstered guns on thick utility belts. Here to do the rounds, then gone in their fancy wagons with reinforced rivet-drilled walls.

Granger, an inhouse guard, spent most of his time on his arse. The face file flipped over on Monitor Two at his station: a scrolling record of all the homeless, mental, thieving patrons who'd ever given the library any trouble; washed their socks or cocks in staff kitchen sinks; tucked a book inside their jacket and claimed not to understand the lingo.

Why steal a book written in English, then, genius?

Granger had seen it all. All the weird junk the library had locked in temperature-controlled rooms above. On his orientation tour, he'd seen shit you wouldn't believe. A rare book constructed from the dried husks of tiny fish; an ugly painting torn straight from the heart of a rich family feud, locked away in trust, in the absence of all trust; a famous poem scrawled by a famous drunk on a torn collar to pay for a pub tab.

He would never understand why people thought any of that shit mattered. Yet it was worth millions, apparently. So the Chubbies acted like they were something important.

But it was the inhouse guys who sat on the frontlines. He'd like to see the Chubbies deal with a crazy old bag wearing a threadbare dressing gown, pockets stuffed with stolen sugar sachets, dirty claws going for your earlobes after you challenged her.

Gray was careful to stay on the good side of the Chubbies, though. A bloke like him, fat and slow, he needed strong allies. He sweated each and every quarterly performance review; that wrinkled bitch with crooked eyes who ruled the roost at reception, squinting over her glasses at him. Pen hovering over F for *Fails to meet expectations*. That report went to his private security firm—she could get him fired, and she hated him, and she loved it.

But the Chubbies file a report, too. And every quarter, Charlie ticked the good box and winked. 'See you Friday night, Gray? Broncos are gonna show Thurston how the game's played.'

'I'll lay in the coldies, mate.'

Friday Night Football, and Gray the only single male in security, so he hosted. Half a dozen blokes usually showed up to his Bracken Ridge flat, expecting beer and pizza and an absence of womenfolk. It was his one regular social contact, and it was worth it. In the ad breaks, sometimes, the Chubbies would brag about some of the stuff they'd seen on the job. Hacked alarm systems, holes drilled through concrete, ram-raided ATMs.

Not at the library. Banks, shopping centres. Places where stuff actually *happened*. When he asked them about the library, they laughed. Gray knew they were laughing at him.

'The only thing that happens at libraries is people crime, mate—nutters going off and wrecking stuff. We just gotta show up now and then, show the mad bastards whose boss. No live action, just prevention. It's a limp dick job, a filler.'

The game comes back on, the video ref spins and flips and flashes a big red NO TRY. The guys hoot in protest.

Gray ignores their jibes, laughs along, sips his beer. *People crime*, hey? Interesting way of putting it.

Her skin told the story of the past year and a half.

At first, just a faint tingling when she would walk through reception, her body catching what her mind missed, all caught up in giddy career dreams. Her lanyard a proud tag of success—she put it on at home in the morning and took it off there in the evening; wore it all the long busride to and fro—she'd simply swipe it through and head upstairs, oblivious.

But then one morning as she chatted with the receptionist, she caught him watching her with terribly careful eyes. It was then her tingling skin began to crawl, up and down the ladder of her ribcage.

Next, he started up the stare game, and her neck would flush and itch each morning. His chair would squeak as he leaned back, and then she'd feel it: his eyes on her behind. She invested in a long drape cardigan, a formless black cloak, and wore it every day.

With recent events, her skin had begun to roast and crisp with rage. Strafed by shingles, furious welts under her bra strap.

Maddy avoided seeing Dr Richards. This issue was not about her *illness*; she craved some anonymity, some release from the safety net woven by the clinic and entangled around her every move. She just needed some damn ointment. Something to stop the itching that cut like blades through to her bones.

So she booked in on a day when she knew Dr Richards was away.

Dr Gale had kind brown eyes but wore outrageous shoes: bright leather clogs with ornamental bows.

Stress-related, Dr Gale had said, and asked her if anything was wrong. So Madeleine tried to explain. That a man at work looked at her funny, watched her all the time.

'All the time?'

'When I arrive in the mornings, he's always there. At his desk. Staring.'

Dr Gale glanced at Madeleine's file displayed on the monitor built into the desk, set at an angle that only doctors could see. Madeleine knew what it meant when strange doctors glanced at her file, knew what it said about her there: distorted cognition, faulty causal reasoning, ineffective coping strategies. Powerful labels that far outshone the subsequent notes of 'partial recovery' and 'ongoing support'.

She pulled down the sleeves of her jumper all the way to the grated quick of her fingertips. Folded herself into her collarbones, made as small a target as possible.

'You say he's a security guard. Doesn't he stare at other people, too?' An insidious boa of doubt twisted around the doctor's words.

Maddi blinked, confused. 'But he stares at *me*.'

'Do you think maybe it's just part of his job?'

That was all it took. Madeleine's precious construction of events—a year of gut-sick instinct and hypervigilance and sleepless nightmares, working out the what and the why so she could stave off the when and the how—collapsed.

And the cursed stone came back.

Near South Brisbane train station, there's a flower stall. A smear of bright colours, angel shapes, sweet soapy smells in the dim filth of the pedestrian underpass. Every morning Granger walked by, and every evening too, five days a week.

He loved her hard as speeding metal. One time at the Archerfield Motorway pre-race show he saw them drop a car from a full-sized crane, the mighty Holden Commodore crushing the Ford below. It was just like that, when he first saw her. Practically tiptoeing past, she crashed into his bleary world.

The ID swipe brought up her name, every morning, five days a week. Madeleine. Sounds like that waterfall, a hidden surprise drumming and singing near the litter-filled picnic ground he went to for family reunions, back when he stayed in touch. Sounds French, like perfumed sex on stiletto heels.

Sounds like the hard rush of his blood when she murmured hello.

He refused the weekend shifts, the night shifts, where the money is. He wanted to be there to greet her each morning. Those two minutes that she's in his sector, it is worth more than overtime, more than any money, more than his pathetic life.

Every morning, her picture flashed up at him when she swiped her card. The ID swipe, her name and picture on Monitor One, right there in front of him. And every morning, he stopped himself from clicking on the link to her employee file. He wanted to find out if anyone could trace it if he did, but didn't know who to trust enough to ask. Meanwhile, it wouldn't be wise to take the risk.

Self-control. See?

He liked that picture. It was surely okay for him to look at it whenever he felt the urge—no harm, no foul. He just had to keep track of things, make sure he could justify it. A few times a day, okay. Once an hour, maybe. Definitely do not leave that picture open, sitting there on his monitor, her eager eyes twinkling up at him all day.

It was a lovely picture, though. Irresistible. Most people looked stiff or sick or stupid in their staff ID photos, but not her. She was carrying more weight then, sweet guinea pig cheeks lifted above a self-conscious smile. A pale pink shirt she still wore sometimes that makes her skin look like marshmallow. Like she would collapse into icing sugar at the first press of his tongue.

His mouth watered every time he looked at that picture.

Then one morning, without thinking about it, without realising he'd been planning that day for nearly a year, he clicked on the forbidden link. And suddenly her home address was right there in front of him. His heart bumped his ribcage in surprise; he squeezed his eyes shut as he killed the file. But it was burned onto the back of his brain, he couldn't forget it.

21/43 Hilldark Road. Her age, his age. It was a sign.

He did nothing about it for a month. He worked, drank, slept. Tried not to dream.

Then he walked past that damn stupid flower stall and got the idea and reached for his wallet before he could think it through. And there it was, just the most beautiful bunch of flowers he had ever seen. The softest and prettiest old-fashioned roses, pale pink and perfumed with sweet milk, just like her. He knew two things from the start: he was smart enough to love her, and he wasn't smart enough to have her.

When they first met, when she first stepped though those giant sliding doors, something about her had caught his eye. She was tentative, putting on a brave front.

He'd demanded her ID, strung with a blood red lanyard around her long, delicate neck. She'd leaned forward over the counter to show him the card, on that first day, holding her silky hair back with one hand so he could read the pass clearly. Blonde hair, brown hair, he couldn't say. Somewhere perfectly in between.

And some days when she wore a certain shade of red, a classy and pale lip-tint red, then her hair was blonde and brown and copper, too, just a little. Hot water pipe hair.

So that first day when she leaned in, held back her hair, elbows awkward, thinking of something else, that's when he caught the scent of her. She smelled how pink looked. She smelled of white chocolate and roses.

So he sent her the roses, anonymously. He was smart enough to know that much, for sure: she wouldn't like getting flowers from him, an older man with his gut bulging over his trousers. He rubbed his knuckles thoughtfully as he directed the florist where to send them. Hilldark Road. He wouldn't say from who, that would ruin it. But it was time to let her in on the world's most powerful secret: that she was loved.

Loved hard.

They were there on her doorstep when she got home from the movies one night: wilted, faded roses, flattened and dying on her doormat.

Terrifying.

She'd stepped over them, unlocked her door, locked it behind her, and headed straight to her bedroom closet. Slid open the door, climbed right into the back. Pushed the door noiselessly shut with her foot, and sat, unmoving; puffer in one hand, keys in the other. Didn't say or think or do anything. Come the dawn, she climbed out to put on rubber gloves and sunglasses. Cleaned her front porch in swift, methodical silence. The she sprayed everything with Glen20, even her hands.

· · ·

'Good morning.' Granger seemingly spoke to the air, to the half dozen staff traipsing in, caffeine-hungry zombies. Yet it was meant only for her, and they both knew it.

Madeleine opened her mouth to deal him a cutting reply, but a rush of bile burned the bird hollow at the base of her throat and she couldn't make a sound. Her body was rebelling against the tearing away of her hide, layer by layer, until she was skinless before him. A slice of sashimi.

She hurried past and avoided the stairs, heading to the lifts, hoping for a quick getaway. The one working lift was on the top floor. As new as it appeared, this building had aged prematurely in the flood; joints creaking, vital systems failing. She pressed the call button and waited, her lungs a shallow bowl of turbulence. Waited, gaze locked on the light panel, periphery focused on her rearguard. Tried not to feel she was trapped here, splayed in a tile and glass box for his pleasure.

Finally, the lights tracked the lift downwards, silver armour coming to save her. Level Four, Three.

It stopped short.

A wave of bloodlessness swept over her, the same sensation as when her mother brushed her bum-length hair as a little girl. One long, long sweep of her nanna's horsehair brush with the tapestry cover, soft against her scalp, down along her spine all the way to the back of her thighs; her barometer sank, the pressure in her veins falling away with a swoon.

She pressed her hands to the sides of her ribcage, forcing the air out to let some more in. Each breath felt thinner, dirtier. She struggled to focus as the lift machinery whirred back into action.

Two.

A loud clunk, and it paused again. Her heart shrank into a tiny, quivering ball. Occasionally, someone was trapped in the lift. She reached for her puffer and gripped it in her hand, out of sight in her bag. She hated using it in front of Granger. In fact, she hated using it front of anyone now. She'd tried hiding in the toilets at work, but the open-plan open-floor open-door policy meant the Men's and Women's shared an entrance before dividing into private cubicles, and that did her in.

The swoon threatened her last remnant of vision; autopilot took the controls. Her right hand raised the blue plastic device, depressed the canister and inhaled deep. Timed perfectly, the medicated gas brought instant relief. Madeleine opened her eyes, lungs pregnant with breath. As she dropped the puffer in her bag, she saw him. He was staring at her, had been watching her the whole time; watched her open lips wrap around the tube. His own mouth moved wetly in ecstatic mimicry.

Ping.

No, she didn't know who sent the flowers, not for a fact. But deep in her brain stem, a decision was made.

That day she rode the lift was her last day before three weeks' annual leave for the summer. She laid her plans well; told her family that she was going away with girlfriends, her girlfriends that she was going away with family.

She had no plans, just needed time alone.

At first, she had talked about the situation with her friends. Back when her skin merely crawled, before it began to tan and tear. *One of the guys at work is pissing me off, being weird.*

Sal rolled her eyes, *yeah, me too. My boss seems nice but he's a real user, makes big promises to everyone, gets me to do the work, then he takes all the credit.* Chose a patchwork mini-dress off the rack at the young designers market. *Men. When will they ever grow up?*

Madeleine quickly learned that her problem was not visible to other people: it lacked solidity. When she tried to pin it down, her words slipped around and became wedged somewhere between paranoia and vanity. She couldn't describe the texture and size of what was happening, couldn't quantify its cost. It was too pervasive, invisible, impossible to define. Worthless.

After the flowers, she stopped mentioning it at all. Packed the whole situation into a hastily refurbished room in the back of her mind, one she had years ago carefully closed and locked and declared abandoned. A bold squatter, every day it arrived with new items of furniture. Big, heavy stuff.

Men had not been her problem. She was as okay with guys as she was with anyone. And she liked just about everyone, since she'd begun to feel well. At uni, her friends would get blind wasted trashed, disappear an hour and reappear with a guy hovering, then throw up on the train home. Crazy stuff. But not her. She had touched the heat too many times when she was sick, had ventured beyond the bounds of safe society and lived to never tell the tale. She was content with a conversation, never gave her number.

But this guy? This guy was not a man at all. He was a monster in the moat, scaring the living crap out of her every day with such skilful sleight of hand that no one suspected a thing.

She delighted in the freedom of her covert home-alone holiday. Four whole weeks in her tiny, beautiful apartment; a permanently pristine tile and glass kitchen, a bathroom with a mirror that lit her skin as if for surgery, a lounge/study nook, a chaste bedroom, and a balcony large enough to fit a banana lounge and a potted geranium. It was next to the train line, affordable. She was safe here. Her parents approved it because there were two other girls living on this floor, just like her, new job holders who still dressed like students.

Instinct kicked in, pumped a constant stream of protective hormones into her thin blood and blocked the narrow canal along which her thoughts once passed from right to left hemisphere, left to right.

Instinct. She developed the food rules, the exercise rules, the vacuuming rules; the rules that stilled her hand and mind. She shut down her online life, account by account, until all that remained of her was a digital slip of a thing, a nano-particle, a generic info@work email account buried inside a labyrinth of firewalls and bureaucracy.

Instinct. She built compartments in her mind, one for administering the rules, one for judging her compliance. And a huge buried chamber for strategic processing. Scenario planning, they called it at work. *If he does this, then I'll do that. If he does that, then...*

And hoping so hard he does do something, something real and concrete and out loud in shared reality. Then she would emerge from the shadow dimension where he had her captured and detained. Colleagues would meet her eye and say *yes, we always knew there was something not right about him.* Maybe even, *you poor thing,* one hand rubbing warmth between her shoulder blades as the other passed a tissue.

Timid steps on the tile stairs. The barber-pruned hairline at the base of Granger's skull prickled, alert to every sign of her. He'd noticed a pheromonal bond grow between them, could sense the air change when she came into his realm. He knew that Madeleine felt it too, and it scared her, the strength of it.

He could watch her almost anywhere in the building.

Watch her movements, memorise her pathways. He's set limits on how often he watched, ensured variety in his patterns, tended to his regular duties diligently. He wouldn't give away their game.

He had to be so careful with his power. Such a tricky balance to maintain: focused, passive, devoted, indifferent; especially through the rush of seeing her again after her endless fucking Summer holiday. She'd been back a week, but he was still hypersensitive; he'd worked so hard to stay attuned while she was away, nurtured that precious bond in his mind. It was intense, knowing she'd returned to the building.

Calf muscles tense as rocks under his grey uniform, he waited for her to round the curve and enter the gated security walk that would bring her straight past him. Instead, the tapping paused.

He glanced at the monitor, quietly pressed a key, shifted to reception view. Behind him, she stood by the locked door next to the elevators. It led to the ground floor studio, and then to the dock lift. She never used this entrance, she took the internal lift straight down from near her cubicle on Four.

Madeleine took a step towards the studio door, then a step away. Indecisive. He watched her, face impassive, but his guts churning in an agony of wonder. What was she doing? Was she working up the courage to speak to him again? It had been months since he had heard her voice in real life, not just on the occasional call to her extension whenever he found an unattended phone. *Hello, Madeleine Kyle speaking.* Faint, friendly, uncertain. Then he'd hang up. Scraps of her, when he craved a feast.

Granger clocked the details on screen as Madeleine paused by the studio door, mentally working through his checklist. He'd loved that part of his training. How to instantly read and remember height, weight, clothes, facial expression, distinguishing marks, suspicious behaviour. A secret handbook on how to make sense of humans.

Madeleine carried no clipboard today. That was new.

Suspicious behaviour.

In a rush, she swiped her ID card and pushed open the door. It was heavy, a hydraulic counterweight set high to slow egress. You had to really want it, to get through the doors in this hallowed place. For an instant, her brolga poise pressed full-length against the white slab. Two hands. Right shoulder. Breast. Thigh.

His cock twitched.

Just before she disappeared into the concrete corridor beyond, she glanced up at the reception security camera. He jolted in his swivel chair, planted his black vinyl boots firmly on the base to keep stable. He hadn't realised she even knew where the camera was.

Clever girl.

As he watched the screen, she locked eyes with him, her face empty and fine as clean bone china.

Then she was gone.

Her notebook, a simple exercise pad, cost sixty-four cents. She layered the front and back covers, inside and out, with lacquered visions of her dreams. Women: slender, stylish, confident. Striding with briefcases, leading in boardrooms, reading the news, painting and sculpting and drawing and writing and teaching. Images of women interspersed with dream houses: by the beach, in the mountains, a loft apartment in New York.

She'd kept a notebook when she'd been ill, but that notebook was Not Allowed. It had been filled with columns, tiny neat figures of her intake and output; the pages blue and red ink-tattooed in such detail they became braille heavy and malleable. It gave her such a complete sense of order, every atom going into or coming out of her body recorded and tracked and catalogued.

For two years after the clinic, she had worked with a therapist who encouraged her to examine her thoughts, feelings, actions in a daily diary. Together, they would read the entries and piece together the patchwork quilt of her psyche in a way that finally made sense: because she believed x, she felt y, and did z.

It was easy to add some extra information, buried among the journal entries about study, work, dreams. Without even knowing it, she had developed a clever encoded system; complete, ready, in a tidy cupboard at the back of her mind. So when she first went to add this new, illicit information to her notebook, she already had an entire language of hieroglyphs.

A soft layer of guilt had crossed her heart like a heavy quilt falling across a freshly made bed. But she had no choice.

Instead of calories, she kept track of *him*.

A dash meant a glance, an exclamation mark when he spoke to her, or in her presence: often he made comments to customers that projected sideways, bent arrows that lanced her as she quickly paced by:

Nice day for it.

And her skin would contract, become just a fraction too small for her form, split.

Anonymous phone calls were a question mark. And once, when he touched her bag, an asterisk.

That was the intake column. The output column looked like a navigator's chart. The entire library was represented there in a code all her own: each level assigned a letter, each quadrant a number. Security blind spots were a small green circle, because that's how she saw them in her mind.

Small green circles, just one or two on most levels, none on Five, and a half dozen in the dock. Little green lights. Go.

Madeleine strides quickly down the corridor; polished concrete floor, white walls. Like a hospital, or a morgue. She passes the studio and pushes through the first set of double doors, silver trim catching the tail of her cardigan. She pulls it free, holding her breath to keep calm. Keep moving forward, down, away. Through the next doors and into the giant elevator, fit for shifting dinosaurs, waiting for her—the timing is perfect. Down one level and out into another corridor: it slopes here, tilting down past the LMR control room where a circuit board the size of a double-wide vending machine controls the comms between all of the behind-the-scenes, underground staff in the whole arts precinct. Right turn, past the *Quarantine Out* door, and then the *Quarantine In*.

It feels safe, being near these systems of public health control. Safe and so familiar, after nearly two years of exploration.

Around the last turn, down through the last doors and into the dock. First stop: the office.

There's no one around, of course. It's lunchtime, and Lance has headed off to The Joynt for his usual Friday special. She likes Lance. He's a muso, plays guitar in pubs around town. He doesn't mind giving her a hand when she needs to switch around the loading schedule, would tuck away toddler-sized Noah's Arks and faux-bungalows for a week without complaining to her boss.

She freezes and focuses on a sound. Hypervigilant. A footstep?

Something, then nothing.

Runs her hand over the desk. Lance's keyboard,

headphones, pen tray. Her hand falls on a large, solid bar. A comforting, cold shape she had often noticed lying on Lance's desk. The heavy duty stapler: a perfectly innocent piece of office equipment, a perfect weapon. Just in case.

Madeleine leaves the office, moves deeper into the dock.

Behind her, a heavy door closes softly, mechanically.

She spies an open cavity past the stacked pallets awaiting collection. Speeds up, almost runs towards it.

River Pump Room: Authorised Access Only. Confined Space Permit Area: Log In Required. But the door, usually locked, now stands ajar, giving her access to new arms of the labyrinth. She spins into the entrance and stands for a moment, leaning first left then right, hand on ribs, wasting precious seconds releasing her breath.

Ahead of her, iron plates rest on steel struts that run the length of the cavernous sump room. A low bass thrum resonates through her chest. She hasn't ever been in this room before, but knows it from her research—it was intended for utilities workers armed with hard hats and steel-capped boots. Each step sets off a harsh rattle as the plates shift and settle. Above her head and to the right, a labyrinth of crinkly silver pipes, big enough for a smart car to drive through, spiral around each other in some alien engineering logic. They emanate from the ceiling, far aloft, and wind their way to the end wall almost out of view. She ducks under a low-lying pipe and peers around to find a way forward.

This might work. She could hide here. But she decides to back out and find another way through the dock, just in case.

A fleshy cough reverberates in Lance's office, between her and the main exit.

Her heart responds with a massive pump, so hard it hurts her chest. She creeps forward, deeper into the bay. The iron plates beneath her feet change from solid metal to a sturdy cross-hatch mesh. Beneath lies a high-dive drop into an Olympic pool of murky water. She reaches a thin metal banister quarantining an opening into whatever lies beneath —she can spy a metal ladder, a concrete ledge, and endless dark.

She stares into the depths below her, mesmerized by the ominous pulse that flickers through the shadowed water. A dark thought swims up towards her from the murky depths.

She creeps over the crackling, groaning mesh plates delicately as a bird, learning to hush her movements by balancing along the joints. Her ballet flats communicate the cold hard bars straight through to her soft soles. She crawls over a low silver pipe twice as round as her. Behind it lies a twin pipe, set higher, so she slides through the narrow gap between the two and hunkers down. Carefully places the industrial stapler on the ground and removes the elastic from her wrist, scoops her long hair into a tail and loops it into a ball before fixing it. Picks up the stapler.

Ready.

A backlit shadow appears in the doorway, human-shaped and silent. It moves forward, following the same path she had taken a minute before, then stopping when it reaches the opening into the mire below. Turns a full circle, eyes sliding over her shadowed hiding place.

It's him. He's taken the bait.

The foul air around her and within her turns solid as glass. She is paralysed with fear, stilling all breath or movement less she shatter into a thousand pieces of nothingness, fall through the mesh and be lost in those sewer depths forever.

He turns his head slowly from side to side now; listening, scanning.

She silently counts to ten. When her frozen mind can reach no higher, she counts to ten again.

He moves. Takes a step towards her, then turns. Turns again, and is now facing away. He pauses, places one hand on the thin steel banister, and leans out over the abyss.

She eases herself out from her hiding place, takes a few steps, and ducks behind another pipe. She's closer to him, and still concealed from view. He bends near in two. Grunts as his fat belly is cleaved by the handrail. He seeks her in the darkness below.

It's time.

She consciously gathers every single morsel of rage within her, and sends it into her thighs. Leaps and charges, stapler held banner high.

He has time for a quarter turn, still bent low and off-balance, and then she is upon him. A ram raid. The stapler firing repeatedly into his skull as she bashes and shoves with the great might of terror.

As he falls, he cries her name. But he hits the water before he can finish, so that he manages only Maddi. Her familiar name, fouled by his tongue. The roar and rattle of a freight train begins at the far wall. She yelps with shock. Confusion. Covers her ears and flicks her eyes all around, seeking the source of the noise.

Megalitres of water rush through the pipes all around her, and a pump motor kicks in from below her feet. The murky depths move beneath her. His body disappears from view.

She leans against the railing, unconsciously using it to force stale air out of her lungs. Clears enough room for a short breath in. The pumps stop as suddenly as it started, and the silence drapes heavily over her. She drops the stapler into the pool, and slowly turns to leave. As she walks out over the rattling iron plates, taking less care this time, she gazes curiously into the four dim corners of the room. Nods to herself, as if confirming something she already knew.

Green light.

Just as she reaches the door, she hears a violent rush turbulence below her feet. She looks down through the mesh and feels the world fall away.

His eyes.

He is looking up at her, blood and water running over his face. Big arms slowly flailing, reaching for purchase, reaching for her. She freezes in terror as he catches hold of a low-hanging pipe. He strains to haul himself up and out from the mire, his low moans growling under the rush of sump water.

Panic bursts in her brain, sending adrenalin right down to her feet. She moves, feet pins-and-needles clumsy at first, then picking up speed. Heading for the door. She looks back as she reaches the light, just about to step out into the main hall of the dock. In the shadows behind her rises a shuffling hulk, dripping with gore, groaning with pain. Staring straight at her.

Madeleine races back out the main door of the dock, throat ragged with rasping breaths. He is right there behind her— she can hear his agonised growls as he lurches forward.

No time to escape. She finds a plan ready in her mind. Deploys it.

Through the main door and out into the corridor, she heads straight up the ramp instead of following the exit signs past the Quarantine rooms. Up the short flight of stairs, along the corridor and into the catering area reserved for use by the library café. She looks around, getting her bearings.

There.

A large coldroom unit. Portable, but permanently parked. Dull silver, white doors stencilled with cool blue company signage. A polar bear maybe—it was worn, partially obscured.

She tucks herself into the gap next to the wall at the far end of the unit, mind racing. Come on, she knows this one. Where is it?

She takes a cautious peek around the corner of the unit. He is out of sight, but she is sure she can hear his heavy footfalls approaching, thudding in time with the beat of heart. She finds the heavy steel handle that vacuum seals the cold room. Pulls on it with all her strength. Immoveable. She places her two hands around it and does not merely pull but leans away, shoes pressed against the lip of the unit wall for purchase. Nothing.

Her eyes twitch with confusion now. Should she run or have one last try? She hears him reach the top of the stairs, and grips the handle in panic. Scans the metal lever under her palm from end to end, and finds a small catch holding it in place. Flicks it out from under the handle and wrenches it free. The door opens and she steps inside without hesitation. Slips off one shoe, supple as snakeskin in her hand, and uses it to prop the door very slightly open. Escape route.

Chilled dark fills the coldroom interior. She moves past the shelves of bagged fresh produce, and into the depths of the unit. Shudders uncontrollably with freezing fear. Finds a hiding place amidst the stacked boxes of cans and bottles. Her breath is all but gone. She waits.

He enters the catering area, and shuffles cautiously towards the coldroom. Pauses. A moment later, one finger probes through the gap on the door, then his hand, then his whole arm. He wrenches the door open with a cry of anger, and launches himself at her.

Madeleine lets out a rough bleat of terror as he heads straight for her.

But Granger misses his step. His big, clumsy feet slip

when they hit the coldroom floor, and he topples. He grabs at the shelves, ripping desperately at whatever he can reach to try and keep his balance. Onions and lettuce leaves and tomatoes cascade around him as he falls. A stack of pumpkins teeters then drops, hitting the floor like gunfire, splitting their sunset spiderweb guts all over his pale blue shirt.

Amidst the crashing chaos, a detail catches her eye. His shirt seems completely dry. How can that be? She flicks her vision clear, checks again. Pale, dry, blue cotton. In need of an iron, splattered with pumpkin gizzards, but dry.

Crack.

His head hits the hard floor and it's now or never. She pushes off the back wall. Takes three tiny steps as a run up, then launches herself at the door. Leaps as high and far as she can, diving as if into a pool towards escape.

Slow motion.

The thrashing body beneath her moans. He reaches up with shaking arms; fingernails scraping along her shins as she glides over him. Her skin tears in long strips from thigh to ankle but she flies over him, out the door, landing on hands and knees. Terror flashes through her muscles, and she pushes herself upright. She twists around and grabs the door, pushing it shut as quickly as she can. A pressure starts to push back against her, but before he can gain any purchase from the inside, the lever clicks into closing position. Her cold-numbed fingers scrabble for the latch, and she locks it into place.

Through the walls of the cold unit, she hears a terrorised howl, and dull thudding against the door. It's drowned out by the pounding in her head, keeping time with her frantic pulse. She quickly cross-checks the high corners of the catering room against the map she holds in her mind. This room is clear, but the corridor in and out is monitored.

Orange light.

She leans down, slides her palms up under her dark denim skirt, presses them to the long cuts stinging the flesh of her thighs. Her hands are hungry for the warmth of her own blood, to bring her senseless fingertips back to life. She presses for a moment to stem the flow, then brings her hands up to check the damage.

Clean. Not a trace of blood. For a moment, her heartbeat hangs in midair. The howls from the cold room soften to a moan, and then fade away to nothing.

She strides over to the landing and stands at the top of the concrete steps. Reaches up to remove her hairband, in one smooth movement sliding it out and slipping it over her wrist. Shakes her hair free and presses the top knuckles of her fingers against her hairline, near her temples. Lifts them an inch clear, and knocks them into her skull. Again and again. She loses time, looking down at the blank corridor, knocking sense into herself. The pain is comforting—she knows it is real. And she can control it. She can stop it any time and the pain will cease, miraculously. A magic trick, a very mild superpower that she mastered at such a tender age: she doesn't see it as the ability to hurt herself, but the strength to save herself.

A small glass dome rests in the corner of the ceiling. She feels its robotic gaze upon her, wonders for a second whether Monitor One in reception is still unattended. Whether anyone has noticed the guard's prolonged absence.

How long has it been?

She takes a slow breath, forcing in the stale air of the dock. It's like crystalline growths attach themselves to her bronchial passages. It hurts.

Madeleine steps down, and reaches the junction in the

corridor. Back into the dock, or turn left and head back aboveground. Her mind is a flickering cascade of images, maps, coded symbols. She reaches deep within, down through the waterfall of chaos, into the farthest basement room of her mind. Neuron pathways flicker and disintegrate as she struggles to separate real from imagined, terror from horror. Shards of consciousness focus into a beam of light, searching for a plan.

At first, there is nothing. Her breath shallows with panic so that her whole torso is still, only the cups atop her clavicles lift delicately with the slightest sign of life.

From behind her, a click. A step. A groan.

She turns left. Ten paces along the corridor towards the elevator, past the *Quarantine In* door, ten paces more. Behind her, the footsteps are speeding up, becoming a determined shuffle. Too close.

She ducks into the small recess with a low ceiling. It houses the Lighting Protection Test Point, a foot-square brass panel like an oversized plaque in a crematorium. She's done her research, knows exactly how much power surges behind it. A lightning bolt, frozen behind the panel, just waiting for a fork to prod it into whiplash action.

Madeleine dives into her pocket and pulls out her keys, fingers deftly finding the largest object on the ring. She reaches for the brass panel set at waist height into the white plaster wall, jams her private post box key into the cleft between the panel and the plasterboard. Twisting up, down, round and round, the ligaments of her thin wrists searing with effort. A coin of plasterboard crumbles and collapses; the panel shifts and pops out just enough. She presses her cheek against the wall and peers through the tiny crack.

A vivid Medusa lurks within. Red and white, black and blue, green and yellow wires hang in orderly ropes beaded into a grey plastic masterboard. She presses her thumbnail against the panel and worms her thumb through up to the second knuckle. She ignores the brass edge as it cuts her to the bone, and levers enough space to push her slender fingers in, probing the interior with her key.

A footfall on the stairs. Too close, too close.

She angles her key at the nearest wire cluster. Hooks a red one, dragging it carefully out through the gap. Carefully pries it loose, just enough to wind it once around her finger. Then presses her spine against the wall so the panel is hidden, keeping her fist of wire nestled in the small of her back. She waits. Her blood is mineral water, thin and salty with anticipation.

Granger rounds the corner, face blanched with confusion, eyes black with pain. Otherwise unmarked.

Madeleine blinks, her brain convulsing with shock waves. She fights a blackout, temples aching with the muscular effort. Wrenches her eyes open to see him standing before her, watching her. His eyes make a meal of her, piece by piece. His fists clench and unclench by his sides.

She forces herself to smile. Just a little.

He smiles back; a lonely, mean kind of smile, all snaggled teeth and dingo breath. Madeleine holds herself completely still as he lifts one hand towards her, wirehaired knuckles reaching for her face. Within an inch of her skin, at the pulsepoint where jaw meets earlobe, he pauses.

She smiles again, broadly this time, and arches her back a little. His hips twitch in response. His hand moves the final distance to touch her skin. As he gently slides his fingers along her chin, her skin tingles and flares.

Agony.

She raises her hand to meet his own. Slowly, carefully, her raw fingertips find his wrist, his forearm. At her touch, his eyes fall shut with a wave of excitement.

As he swoons, Madeleine swoops. She clamps her fingers

tight around him and spins to wrench the wiring free. He lunges towards her. She uses his momentum to pull him close, then slips aside. Lets his weight ram up against the wall. Drags the ragged end of red wire into his armpit.

As she jumps clear, she sees the power bite, feels it throw her back against the opposite wall. He shoots out his other arm to push off against the wall but lands on the brass panel. Closes the circuit.

A brilliant ray arcs around his torso. The overhead lights dim, then fail. She is caught at midnight, the only light a freakish solar flare in the shape of a man. Time hangs, bright in an infinite darkness.

A sickly yellow shimmer blinks from above. It strengthens and bleaches as the generator kicks in.

His epileptic gaze—expressionless, morbidly intense—locks on her face. He still dances for her, and she watches, gasping air putrid with the taste of his meat.

She turns away as he slumps to the floor, his clothes smoking, his left flank blackened as a barbecue plate. Her mind is clear, an empty exhibit locked under a Perspex display.

Weak, she leans against the wall to support each step. Flicks up her gaze, confirming what she already knows. No camera in this recess. But as soon as she steps into the main corridor, the robotic eye is on her.

Red light.

Her feet turn to the one place she feels safe. Barely conscious, she moves slowly, drunkenly down the corridor.

She slides under the roller door, a whisper of cardboard the only evidence of life in the dock. Crawls to the shelving unit, her old friend, and wrenches herself up to standing. She can't feel her legs; her feet drag pigeon-toed beneath her as she pulls herself along towards safety.

A deep, angry moan sounds from Dock Control. For a second, she lets herself imagine that it is Lance, shocked and outraged, rushing to her defense.

But even in its extremis, she knows that voice. And that's not Lance.

Terror strikes rictus through her whole body. For a moment she stands as rigid and grey as the steel corner post of the shelving unit. Her arm slowly finds the power of movement, reaching out to the wall. She stumbles with relief into her hidey-hole. The shelves are full of boxes; she knows she is, for now, invisible. Mind is empty of options, protective instincts spent, she slumps down into a ball.

On autopilot, her fingertips find a familiar friend. They follow the rough concrete grain along until a bolt head nestles in her palm. They twist and jiggle the bolt, and the comfort of the familiar sends a wave of surrender through her.

Shuffling footsteps approach. Black boots at the roller door. Fat fingers grasping the grubby rim, grunts of effort as the door is pulled and jerked open a short way, then sticks.

'Madeleine?' Granger's face appears underneath, peering into her inner sanctum. Groaning with frustration, he rolls onto his back and squeezes his torso through.

Her heart hammers painfully in her chest, the only thing she can feel in her otherwise numb body. Her mind is still locked away, far from reach.

He worms his way into the chamber, grunting and sweating with the effort. Supine, he propels himself along the floor by bending up his knees, digging in his heels and shoving his giant bum forward until his legs straighten. Again, again, until his whole body is in the chamber. He tries to roll over, but his fat gut slows him down. He rocks his elbows back and forth to get the necessary momentum.

She looks down upon him, writhing on the floor like a giant wounded blue-tongue lizard. Sudden sensation flashes through her body, her mind snapping awake, legs straightening underneath her. Her hands tighten their grip on the shelves, and she pushes, wedging herself between the back of the shelves and the wall, using the leverage. The shelves topple forward. She lets out a scream of victory, suddenly stifled as the shelves rock back, threatening to mash her against the wall.

She braces her feet flat against the wall and shoves with the last of her strength. As the shelves begin to tip, boxes slide to the floor and she is left exposed. He sees her and yells —unintelligible, pleading—as she catches the upper shelves and simply hangs there.

He scrambles to his knees, reaching for the corner post. Too late. Madeleine jumps to one side, watching in fascination as the metalwork finally topples past the point of no return. Then she turns and runs towards the stairs, her escape. As her right foot hits the bottom step, something grabs at her left. An excruciating crunch; her ankle is caught and held.

The heavy shelves crash down, crushing boxes, bodies, everything.

Madeleine drifts awake, but her eyelids stay shut, too heavy to lift. She can smell the musty eucalypt tang of blood. Her leg. Snakebite, car crash, she's uncertain; but the wrenching sting of it has forced her awake. She becomes aware of a noise—a faint scratching, a rodent sound, a cockroach scuttle. She needs help. Opens her mouth to call. Lungs empty, her diaphragm convulses with a single, silent weep.

She is trapped on her stomach, chest flattened painfully against the floor, arms pinned underneath.

She pours her energy into vision instead, wrenching her eyes open. A grey chamber. She twists around a little, wincing as her brow scrapes along the concrete. A long, long way away she sees a foot, trapped under a fallen mess of steel posts and heavy clapboard shelving. The foot is wearing one of her shoes.

A gargling groan startles her from the far side of the chamber. Madeleine turns her head again, vision blurring from the effort. She makes out a pale blue uniform in her peripheral vision.

A rasping whisper drifts across the chamber, surrounds her.

I will save you. I will save you. I will save you.

A chilling wave of anger surges through her limbs. Her ribs contract sharply, then expand, forcing a cloud of stultifying air into the vacuum of her lungs.

No!

She hears a feeble tapping and then a clumsy burst of static. His radio.

The Chubbies will come. His voice gurgles, full of phlegm.

They won't come. She has seen his pathetic greetings ignored by those men, cocksure as the pistols at their belts. *They hate you.*

While she talks, she painfully works one of her trapped hands up towards her throat. Her fingers find the fine chain, and follow it until they make contact with a smooth plastic sphere. She triggers the alarm, draws another sandpaper breath.

Paramedics. Her ragged voice swells with triumph.

But—. He stops, spits, and groans. *Why?*

She turns her head away, finished with him.

They lie in silence, the only sound a terrible dripping

cough from his side of the chamber, like a sucking geyser getting ready to blow.

In the distance, an engine rumbles. A prolonged metallic creak reverberates throughout the Dock as the outer door is triggered open. They both wait as the engine chugs deeper into the Dock then slows outside their chamber, shifting gears for a three-point-turn.

Madeleine lies mute, immobile, nearly blind. Drained of all energy, her systems are closing down, one by one. She cannot feel the concrete floor beneath her cheek. Her thoughts writhe with rage at this body that has always, always failed her. But she is still awake within, and waits, ready for the sound of the roller door opening. Longing for the efficient economy of paramedics. She's seen them in action enough times to be able to predict their movements perfectly.

The engine stays running. A commercial radio jock burbles in the background. The chamber door creaks, and jams. She tries to call out, but is trapped in the recurring nightmare where you run and run and your feet don't move.

Someone curses. Footsteps slouch away from the door over towards Dock Control. The sickly sweetness of blue muffler smoke unfurls itself under the roller door, sliding its fingers over her mouth, down her throat. Suffocating.

A dying murmur bleats nearby. *Ambos? Chubbs?*

She can feel his hope, his last gasp. Even in his last moments, he seeks to steal from her an uninvited intimacy.

Neither. She moves her mouth, uncertain if she is making any noise. From the far end of the shelves, a wet whisper strains, then fades quickly to nothing.

She hears one single, hollow cough, and then the compost smell of death is at her nostrils.

Madeleine drifts into the deepest region of her mind. Arms, legs, belly, chest—her whole being—cut adrift from consciousness as she gently sinks to the place she knows so well. It is dark, and calm, and safe down there.

Her pulse races light and fast until it burns itself out; her prone body becomes entirely still, face down on the chamber floor.

Jeeziz fucking kerist.

Lance yanks the roller door up in one shove to see Granger's crushed torso lying in a pool of liverish blood. A flash of pale pink fabric, so out of place in this awful scene, catches his eye from across the chamber.

Fuck me. A second man joins Lance. *Carnage.*

You check him. Lance points down, then steps carefully over gore-stained boxes to where Madeleine lies.

This one, oh, his guts are ... everywhere. Gross. The delivery guy stares at Granger, fascinated. *His legs are mashed... the shelves... then his body's over here. Fuck, dude, he's been cut in half!*

Shut up. Get on the phone. There's been an accident. Lance bends over Madeleine, tears of shock pricking his eyes. He puts his ear to her face.

Nothing.

A siren wails outside, getting closer, tyres squealing as they race into the dock.

She's not breathing, Lance says. *Shitshitshit.* He lays his head on the ground, prayer position, nose to nose with her ghostly face.

And then he sees it. A tiny drumbeat, pulsing in the taut lilac skin over her temple.

The rhythm of her life.

ACKNOWLEDGMENTS

Thank you to Varuna House and Queensland Writers Centre who supported me to write and develop this story, to Matt Lamb and Phil Crowley - the first editors to believe in my work– and to publisher extraordinaire, Peter M. Ball. And a huge thanks to my partner Luke and sons Declan and Griffin who all enthusiastically love and support my art tornado.

Thank you also to SLQ staff who helped me understand its hiding places. Coincidentally, as I was researching and writing this story, a senior manager was secretly taking and sharing obscene, invasive photographs of women and girls visiting the library. When discovered, he left the job and was not prosecuted.

I believe abuse survivors know when abuse is occurring around us: we develop a creep radar, because we know the legal system often fails to protect us. So, thank you to everyone with a creep radar who has shared their stories with me: I hope this one gives you great satisfaction.

ABOUT THE AUTHOR

Meg Vann trekked over glaciers with her toddler while pregnant, talked herself out of being mugged on the streets of New York, and was detained for no apparent reason at Uzbekistan airport while on a diplomatic visa.

A crime writer, publisher, and scholar, and an abuse survivor, Meg has been making up thriller stories since before she could read and write. She seeks to confound assumptions about women's criminality and victimhood as part of a broader cultural understanding of gendered violence and the menace of intimacy.

Meg established the Maher Fellowship for Women Writers for regional and Indigenous women to access creative writing development. She is an active member of Australian Crime Writers Association and Sisters in Crime, is the former CEO of Queensland Writers Centre, and regularly appears at writers festivals.

Find out more at megvann.com

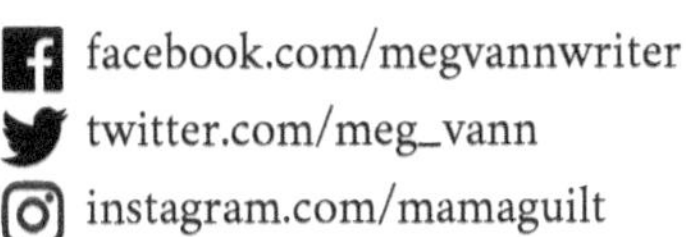

facebook.com/megvannwriter

twitter.com/meg_vann

instagram.com/mamaguilt

www.ingramcontent.com/pod-product-compliance
Lightning Source LLC
Chambersburg PA
CBHW030846200726
48285CB00007B/2575